BEAR PLAY

PICTURES AND WORDS BY
MIELA FORD

GREENWILLOW BOOKS, NEW YORK

The full-color photographs were reproduced from 35-mm slides.
The text type is ITC Kabel Medium.

Printed in Hong Kong by South China Printing Company (1988) Ltd.
First Edition
10 9 8 7 6 5 4 3 2 1

Library of Congress Cataloging-in-Publication Data
Ford, Miela.
Bear play / by Miela Ford.
p.   cm.
Summary: Two polar bears play in the water.
ISBN 0-688-13832-2 (trade).   ISBN 0-688-13833-0 (lib. bdg.)
[1. Polar bear—Fiction.   2. Bears—Fiction.]   I. Title.
PZ7.F75322Be   1995   [E]—dc20   94-25739   CIP   AC

For Aurora and Yukon,
the polar bears who live
in the Seneca Park Zoo

Let me think.

What can I do?

I'll call a friend.

We'll play in the water

together.

Up

and down.

Look!

A ball.

Can I get it?

Watch me try.

I got it with my nose and toes.

Now I'll throw.

Get ready.

Here it comes.

Good catch!

You have to go?

We had fun.

We'll play again tomorrow.